First published in Great Britain in 1990
by Simon & Schuster Young Books

Simon & Schuster Young Books
Simon & Schuster International Group
Wolsey House
Wolsey Road
Hemel Hempstead
Herts. HP2 4SS

Printed and bound in Belgium by Proost International Book Production
Set in 16pt Optima bold educational by
Goodfellow & Egan Phototypesetting Limited, Cambridge

British Library Cataloguing in Publication Data
Lewis, Rob
   Ollie's Song
   I. Title
   823'.914 [J]

ISBN 0-7500-0200-X
ISBN 0-7500-0201-8 Pbk

Ollie's SONG

written and illustrated by
Rob Lewis

SIMON & SCHUSTER

LONDON • SYDNEY • NEW YORK • TOKYO • SINGAPORE • TORONTO

Ollie came running home from school.
He was very excited.
There was going to be a talent competition.
You had to do something you were good at
on stage in front of the parents.
'I'm going to be in a competition!'
yelled Ollie.

'What are you going to do?' asked his mother.
Ollie hadn't thought of that.
'I'm going to be a magician,' said Will.
'I'm going to juggle,' said Lucy. 'Anyway,
Ollie's too young to be good at anything.'
Lucy was right. Ollie couldn't think of
anything he was good at. He couldn't juggle
and he couldn't do tricks.
'Why don't you sing a song?' said his mother.

'Yippee! A song! A song!' sang Ollie. 'I'm going to sing a song in the competition.'

He went off to write some words.
Then he hummed a tune to fit.
'Now you must learn the words and practise
singing the tune,' said his mother.

So Ollie practised.

Lucy was balancing a club on her beak.

'That's skilful,' said Ollie.

'It's concentration,' said Lucy.

Will was busy pulling rabbits out of hats.

'That's clever,' said Ollie.

'It's magic,' said Will.

Horace was zooming.

'What are you doing, Horace?' asked Ollie.

'I'm doing an aerobatic display,' said Horace.

'That's brilliant,' said Ollie.

'It's careful timing,' said Horace.

Esme was covered in flour.
'I'm going to show people how to make a pie,'
she said.
'That smells tasty,' said Ollie.
'It's good mixing,' said Esme. 'Now keep
your beak out of the bowl.'

Ollie was glum.
Everyone's act was better than his.
He couldn't get his tune right and
he kept on forgetting the words.

At last the day came for the competition.
A special stage had been made
and all the parents had come to watch.

Ollie was very nervous.

First, Lucy did her juggling and balanced
a club on her beak while standing on one leg.
Everyone clapped.

Horace did his aerobatics and did a loop-the-loop.
Everyone gasped.

Will did his magic and sawed someone in half.
Everyone cheered.
Esme made an enormous pie and covered the
parents in flour.
Every mouth watered.

Ollie was so nervous he didn't want to
do his song.
'Go on, Ollie!'
Lucy gave him a shove.

Ollie tripped on one of Lucy's clubs
and went whizzing across the stage.
Everyone laughed.

'Get back on!' said Will.

He gave Ollie a push.

Ollie skidded on Esme's butter and . . .

landed in Esme's pie.
Everyone roared with laughter.

Ollie couldn't do
his song.
He hid in Will's
magic box.

The magic box sprung
Ollie into the air.

He grabbed the curtain, slid down
and landed on a bag of flour.
Everyone laughed until they cried.

It was time for the competition to be judged.
Ollie sat in the corner on his own.

'Never mind, Ollie,' said Lucy.
'You'll do better when you're older.'
'At least you tried,' said Esme.
'Even if you did ruin my pie.'

Third prize went to Will for his magic tricks.
Second prize went to Esme for her piemaking.
But first prize went to Ollie
for his very funny comic act.

Everyone clapped and cheered and as an encore . . .

Ollie sang his song.

There are more delightful picture books by Rob Lewis for you to enjoy

The Great Granny Robbery
Grannies all over town have been disappearing and the police are mystified. Len the Laugher and his band of evil robbers are responsible for these goings on but where does he take them? And why? Read this thrilling tale and find out!
Hardback ISBN 0 356 11847 9   **Paperback** ISBN 0 356 11848 7

Hello Mr Scarecrow
This simple but vivid story describes a year in the life of cheerful Mr Scarecrow, as he stands in a field through the seasons. Month by month he is visited by different animals and watches the countryside activities that surround him, until his poignant demise.
Hardback ISBN 0 356 11798 7   **Paperback** ISBN 0 7500 0194 1

Friska the Sheep that was too Small
Friska, the smallest sheep in the flock, is teased by all the other sheep. She tries to make herself look bigger but nothing really works. Then one day a hungry wolf finds the flock and Friska has a chance to prove that bigger isn't always better.
Hardback ISBN 0 356 13049 5   **Paperback** ISBN 0 356 13050 9

Come Back Hercules
An original and amusing rhyming story. Hercules the goldfish is dissatisfied with his bowl in the bathroom and escapes down the lavatory! His eventful journey from U-bend to river's end is fraught with danger but all ends happily in a superior fish tank.
Hardback ISBN 0 356 16522 1   **Paperback** ISBN 0 356 16523 X

The White Bicycle
Ravi's rusty old bike would appear to have come to the end of its useful life. Or has it? A tramp, a runner, a poacher and Joe, the junk shop man find a use for it and so, in the end, does Ravi.
Hardback ISBN 0 356 13794 5   **Paperback** ISBN 0 356 13795 3

You'll Be Late Father Christmas
Written by Lucille Powney · Illustrated by Rob Lewis
With Christmas only days away, Father Christmas has begun to panic. There are so many presents to wrap for so many children . . . it's time to turn to new technology for help. In this hilarious story, Father Christmas discovers that new machines *do* go wrong and he has to call on some old friends to put things right.
Hardback ISBN 0 356 16820 4   **Paperback** ISBN 0 7500 0180 1

Published by Simon & Schuster Young Books and available from all good bookshops